Frankie
the Fly and
His New Friend
Jesus

Missy Byrd

AuthorHouse™
1663 Liberty Drive
Bloomington, IN 47403
www.authorhouse.com
Phone: 1 (800) 839-8640

Published by AuthorHouse 01/12/2018

ISBN: 978-1-5462-2418-1 (sc)
ISBN: 978-1-5462-2417-4 (e)

Library of Congress Control Number: 2018900468

authorHOUSE®

We often say: "If I could be a fly on the wall....". I started thinking about what a fly would see if he were on the wall inside the tomb when Jesus arose from the dead. So my story starts with Frankie the fly. Frankie was a very adventurous fly, who always seem to get himself into situations that could be dangerous. He lived in Jerusalem during the last days of Jesus.

His best friend was a small donkey named Danny. Frankie loved flying and landing on Danny. Danny would walk around giving Frankie a ride when he got tired of flying. They were always together. Danny was walking around in his barn when Frankie came to visit. Landing on the window seal, Frankie says, "Hi Danny!" Danny answered, "Hello Frankie. What have you been into this morning?" Flying towards Danny to land on his ear, "Nothing yet!!" They were best friends so they always loved being together. While Danny and Frankie were enjoying their visit, Danny's owner came into the barn. Frankie hid by Danny's ear while the owner tied a rope around Danny to lead him outside.

Frankie was very fearful of people, fear of being swatted and shew'd by anything people could find. Danny's owner tied him up to a well while he was filling up the water containers. Hiding behind Danny's ear, Frankie noticed two men coming up to the owner. Frankie was curious trying to hear what they were talking about, but being scared of strangers, he ducked behind the ear again. The strangers took Danny's rope and started leading him to the front gate of Jerusalem. Frankie flew off of Danny, but stayed close by to see where he was going. As Danny went thru the gates, Frankie flew up to Danny's ear. "Danny, who are these men?" Frankie asked. Danny replied that he did not know but they were very friendly.

The men lead Danny to a crowd of people. Suddenly, the crowd parted and a man who had such a pleasant and friendly face came up to Danny. Frankie landed on Danny and said, "Danny, who is this man?" Danny said that he didn't know but he really likes him. Frankie said that he heard some of the men call him Jesus. Jesus went up to Danny and began gently petting him. Danny smiled and realized that this Jesus has such a gentle and peaceful spirit. Frankie told Danny that he liked this man called Jesus.

Being scared of people, Frankie was so surprised that he liked Jesus. He knew that Jesus would not hurt him. Jesus gently sat on Danny's back, which Danny did not mind at all. Frankie was also riding by Danny's ears keeping a close eye on Jesus. Thinking to himself, Frankie wondered, "who is this man named Jesus? I have never seen him before in Jerusalem." Suddenly, Jesus looked right at Frankie, but he wasn't afraid. Jesus made Frankie feel comfortable. Jesus smiled and winked at Frankie. Frankie knew that he liked this man called Jesus.

Entering the city of Jerusalem, the people began waving palm leaves yelling, "Hosanna!!" Danny and Frankie enjoyed all of the attention that was happening. Frankie enjoyed riding with Jesus and Danny. Slowly, Jesus got off of Danny's back and returned him to his owner, but they didn't want to leave Jesus. Danny and Frankie looked back at Jesus and Jesus gave them a smile and a wink. "Danny, I really like Jesus didn't you?" Frankie asked. Danny replied, "Yes, I did! Jesus must be a very important man!"

As the days went by, Frankie often thought of Jesus and how he loved being around him that day. He told Danny that he was going to look for Jesus and see if he was still in Jerusalem. He flew into different windows looking for him. Finally, he seen a small window high up in an old house. He landed on the window seal and seen a long table. It was the same men who took Danny to Jesus. Frankie seen Jesus sitting at the table with all of his friends. Jesus was talking to them like he was teaching them. Jesus seen Frankie on the window and winked, he decided that he was not going to leave Jesus's side.

Frankie followed Jesus from that day on. The next day, Frankie flew with the group to a garden. He could tell that Jesus was concerned about something. Watching from afar, Frankie was very curious about why Jesus was sad. Frankie didn't know what to do so he flew back to the city to find Danny the donkey. "Danny, I found Jesus again." Frankie said. Danny said, " Where?" Frankie told him about finding Jesus in a building eating with his friends, then how he followed him into a garden. Frankie told Danny about how he felt sad because Jesus didn't seem happy anymore. Frankie decided to sleep in Danny's barn because he wanted to be with his friend.

The next day, Frankie was going to go back to the garden to see if Jesus was better. He heard loud yelling and seen a large crowd gathering outside of the palace. "Crucify Him!!" they were yelling. Frankie wondered who they were talking about and seen someone with their hands tied in front of him. As he flew closer, he noticed that it was Jesus! He became really angry at the people who wanted this nice man killed. He flew as fast as he could back to Danny to tell him what is going on in the city of Jerusalem. They both were very upset. They were going to lose their new friend that they liked very much. Frankie was so discouraged seeing how mean the people were to his friend.

As the day went on, Frankie followed Jesus through the crowd. Even though he was small, he wanted to protect him. Frankie could not believe how fast the crowd turned on such a nice peaceful man like Jesus. Frankie's heart broke when they put Jesus on the cross. He was so ashamed of the reactions of the people who lived in his city. Sadly, Frankie flew up to Jesus as he hung on the cross. "It's ok Frankie. I know you are sad, but do not be mad at these people. They don't realize what they are doing." Frankie could not believe what he was hearing. After what these people just did him, he said not to blame them?

Frankie stayed close to Jesus, feeling like Jesus's protector. Sitting on top of the cross, he heard Jesus say: "It is finished", then he died. As a tear went down his face, Frankie decided to tell Danny. After flying back into town and to Danny's barn, he told the whole story. Danny could not believe how sad this story is of Jesus. They both cried while talking about their new friend and that now he was gone. Danny said, "Go back to Jesus and find out where they are going to bury him so we can visit." Frankie flew back to the cross, and as he got closer, he noticed Jesus was gone. After he looked around while flying, he seen some people carrying a body that was wrapped in a white cloth. "Could this be Jesus?" He flew closer but could not tell because Jesus's face was covered.

People placed the body inside a tomb and Frankie followed them. Frankie thought he could get a closer look before they closed the tomb. Flying around inside the tomb, he realized that this had to be Jesus. Suddenly it got dark inside the tomb. Frankie did not make it out before they closed the tomb. "Oh no, what am I going to do now?" thought Frankie. As the days went by, Danny started worrying about Frankie. He had not seen him since Frankie stopped by and told him what was happening to Jesus.

By the third day of being trapped in the tomb, Frankie was becoming very weak from not having food or water. He did not think he would ever get out of this situation, and he has found himself in plenty of them. Suddenly, a bright light came from nowhere! Frankie thought someone opened the tomb, but it was still closed. The light was so bright that he could hardly see what was happening. He did see a beam of light shine on Jesus and Frankie was just in shocked of what was happening.

Jesus was moving and suddenly stood up! He was dressed in a white robe and a purple material draped over one shoulder. "Hello Frankie." said Jesus. "Jesus, you were dead but now you are alive!" Frankie said. Jesus said, " Yes, I died for everyone's sins so that they can be free. Now, all you have to do is ask me into your heart and I will forgive you of your sins". Frankie said, "Please come into my heart Jesus." So together, Jesus and Frankie prayed the prayer of salvation. Suddenly an angel appeared and rolled the big stone away that was blocking the entrance of the tomb. Jesus said, "Frankie, now go and tell everyone about me and tell them everything that you have experienced." Frankie could not wait to go and tell Danny about Jesus coming into his heart!

Printed in the United States
By Bookmasters